# From Prostitution to Purity

# From Prostitution to Purity

SAUNDRA ROBINSON

# From Prostitution To Purity

I give glory to GOD for this testimony. He has given me the grace to survive it, the will to conquer it, and the courage to share it. To God be the glory for the afflictions, persecutions, and victories associated with knowing Christ and doing his will. I thank GOD for the protection of my life and the lives of my children. Thank you, LORD, for saving my soul and preserving my physical body. This book is only for the glory of GOD, not to glorify self or sin, but to give hope and deliverance to others.

# Contents

# To the Readers

I pray that your mind and your heart are opened and full of God's love and have compassion towards anyone you may know who fits the description in this book. I strongly suggest that you pray before reading this material.

God inspired me to write this book in order to reveal error in what is said and thought to be natural and acceptable with today's women versus what the word of God says. Also to challenge the ways of Christian women and expose those ways to the light of God's truth and their consequences. To give direction on salvation, along with finding and breaking generational curses.

**I know that in writing this book I may experience some persecution, but I refuse to tiptoe around my testimony at the expense of another person's life. Some folks may even say that I am a fool. The word of God tells me that God uses the foolish things of the world to confound the wise . . . (1 Corinthians 1:27). God was looking for a fool when He called me (phrase spoken by Prophet Kevin Powe).**

*Joshua 6:22  Go into the harlot's house . . . and bring out the woman . . .*

PLEASE DO NOT LEAVE THIS MATERIAL AROUND

YOUNG READERS AS THEY ARE TOO IMPRESSIONABLE.

ALTHOUGH THIS MAY BE A GREAT

COUNSELING TOOL FOR THE KINGDOM OF GOD, IT

CAN BE AN INSTRUMENT OF EVIL IN THE HANDS OF

THE ENEMY. I STRONGLY SUGGEST THAT READERS

BE 18 YEARS OF AGE OR OLDER.

*Joshua 6:22  Go into the harlot's house . . . and bring out the woman . . .*

# The Making of a Harlot—
## It's Premeditated

Being a whore isn't something that just happens, nor do you wake up one day and decide, Today I'm going on a path of whoredom. When I was a child, I never dreamed that that particular lifestyle would become mine; such a thing never entered my mind. First of all, seeds were planted into my life. As far back as I can remember, and from what I was told, women have dominated my family in number and character.

My grandmother was a sweet woman yet in control of everyone and everything. She had five daughters and three sons: three out of eight killed people, another threw lye in a woman's face, and two of them were violent gunslingers that shot several people, so I was told, all in the name of control. My family knew of GOD but had no relationship with him. When I researched my family history concerning GOD, there was no concrete mention other than they knew and ignored the Lord.

I came from a family of unaffectionate and distant people, people who weren't friendly or trusting of family members or outsiders. We were a very self-centered people. It was an every-man-for-himself type of family. We hardly had family gatherings, never a family portrait nor baby pictures, and none of those good old family stories. The more I research my family's history the less the living members knew. They all died fairly young and the rest are scattered like the children of Israel.

I'd like to focus on Mama. Mama was strong, sarcastic, a go-getter, better than Jehu in a fight. A woman who didn't know how to cry, but could humor herself at the first sight of pain, much like myself. Her determination was frightening; she used to say, "I'm hell bent on getting this or that."

Music was Mama's first love. She used it to motivate herself; she used it to put herself in the mood for anything that she wasn't in the mood for. She used music to bring herself comfort, and it would also cry for her. I believe she even got some of her ideals from music. She would also set the mood for others with music. She had a big appetite for various types of music, and I believe music was also a stronghold in her life, depending upon the style of the music and the season it was created in.

I admired ever so much how Mama handled herself and her business. Mama could work her way into, and out of, any type of situation. She always had a business plan. She had several card games weekly, along with fish fries, séances, beef, and beers.

She would sell chances, cook in bars, run her own speakeasy, and so on. You know the routine; Mama was a hustler by nature. Again I really loved the way she handled things, so what I admired became my desire.

Mama was meticulous in her appearance. She actually performed a ritual before making her entrance. Her hair was completely in place strand by strand. Her body was oiled to a shine. Her clothes were the best money could buy. Her shoes fit her character very unique. She smelled like fresh laundry on a bed of roses, and her nails and lips were always red. Mama knew exactly what it took to get the looks. I loved it all, and so I learned how to prepare myself like Mama.

Mama was a thinker; I knew how she thought, because she would always speak her mind to me. She'd never run out of creative ideas or schemes on how to get ahead. She had an original saying for everything, or a philosophy on every issue of life. She'd say things like "If the master came by to buy a nigger, you'd be the first one I'd sell." She would often talk about slow walking a nigger, meaning catching him when his guard was down.

*Joshua 6:22 Go into the harlot's house . . . and bring out the woman . . .*

Mama was a teacher, and GOD knows I was a good student. I learned from Mama how to regulate the pitch of my voice. My phone voice was soft and sweet and kind of proper; my other voices changed from smooth to sexy, to a cute whining, and low-pitch pity, a high-pitch giddy, demanding, and a false firm. Mama's vocabulary was limited, but she didn't do any unnecessary talking anyway, so I learned when to speak and when to listen, how to cuss and when not to.

I also learned how to seduce men with just my language. I could take one innocent statement made by a man, rephrase it in a seductive manner, or reply to it in a seductive manner, and make him either submit to it, blush, or sometimes apologize. Men like women who play word games, or women who tease them.

I learned when to play sick, how to be pitiful, when to cry, and how long to cry, "You know that's important." I learned what to give, how to give it, who to give it to, when it was deserved, how much to give, and at what time and what place.

I learned how to sit, with my legs making a suggestion, how to cross them and how to place my hands on them as if they were in a showcase. How to stand at a sexy ease, stand making a sexy suggestion, how to bend over while standing, how to draw attention when I reached for something while standing. I learned how to work my facial features: I could use my eyes to make suggestions, and I could close them slowly and include a slight body movement that would paralyze any man. I could use them to stare at a man and melt his heart as well as empty his wallet in one blink.

I could squint my eyes to say, "Make your move." My lip movements were easy. I had a lot of choices to learn from. For instance the soap operas brought me great promise along with the movies, and of course Mama. My pucker was always an invitation. The biting of my bottom lip was sending a challenge; my lipstick and lipliner would make any man fantasize.

I learned how to walk. Actually it came along with the rest of the package. What I mean is, it just fell in place. There are different styles of walking; it all depends on where you are and what you are after.

Concerning men, Mama taught me many things as well. The eyes are the windows to the soul, Mama used to say. You have a natural eye that lets you see the surface of things, and the naked eye or spiritual eye where you can see good or evil. Not everyone has a spiritual eye, and it runs in our family, Mama used to say. Mama used to say if you use your naked eye you could see greed, desperation, loneliness, many desires, rejection, and all sorts of weaknesses in people.

Mama would say if you can see these things in men, some men could see them in you. So I taught myself how to be stone faced, plain faced, innocent faced—whatever face it took to disguise my motive, I could make it. My eyes would then fall in place.

So I learned to study men by concentrating and deeply watching their eyes and their body language. Some men didn't require much study because their body movements showed whether they were confident, lazy, weak, strong, ambitious, or nervous and so on. I purposely didn't mention whether or not the men were educated because that doesn't matter when you have a lust, greed, or control issue.

I learned to manipulate a man by noticing how needy he was and identifying the need in him. Finding out his business was important; how he ran his home; how much he spent on bills, haircuts, shoes, and clothes. How he ran his home also meant his taste in furniture and other items. If those things were cheap or expensive, that would tell me much about what I could expect to get out of him.

His work habits were important and all his affairs such as how long he slept on Saturdays, did he wash his own car, whether he picked up after himself—I needed to know all of those things to consider whether or not to invest my time in him.

Finding his weaknesses, what made him tick, what made him sick, what made him tired, what motivated him, what depressed him, what he loves, what he hates, what makes him laugh, and what makes him feel good—all of these things were important in order to gain control.

I remember so clearly Mama giving me direct instructions on a particular man who visited her speakeasy. He was 41, and I was about 14 years old. She said, "He likes you so make him pay just for sitting in your company, and get him to buy some drinks. Whatever you ask him for he'll give it to you." After testing him I was amazed to find out what length he'd go to please me.

Mama taught me not to take expensive gifts, because she said if a man finds out he's being used, he'll take them all back. Just ask for more money than you need, then you'll always have more than enough. I could go on and on about my learning experiences with Mama, but I believe you've got the picture.

*Joshua 6:22  Go into the harlot's house . . . and bring out the woman . . .*

After learning all of this, I hated being a child. I hated being under my mother's control, so I began to act out and got put out. After much time in the streets living from house to house, experiencing cold, hunger, and dehydration, I vowed to myself never to be broke or hungry again.

I went to the neighborhood after-hour spot, and there I met this fairly old man who asked to drive me home. I thought to myself, *Yea, girl, you're going to eat tonight.* So I accepted the ride, and the man began to proposition me. He said, "How much is it to touch your breast?" I said, "Ten dollars." He then stretched out his hand to touch me, but he couldn't. When I looked into his eyes I could see his regret probably because I was so young. He reached in his pocket and pulled out $10 and gave it to me. I can't find words to express how I felt at that time. I remember feeling somewhat sad because of what I was doing and allowing to happen to me. I also felt like I had no choice. He then said, "Girl, go home to your mom." I looked at him with tears in my eyes and said, "I can't." He then opened the door and let me out of the car and pulled off. From that day on I knew there was no need to suffer any longer.

I took on my first sugar daddy, the one I had met at Mama's house, and I moved in with him. He wasn't sweet at all; he was just a dirty old child molester who sweetened the blow with money. I was fourteen when I began to study him and fifteen when I approached him. He was an easy mark, and I played him like a fiddle, so I thought. I was really playing myself.

He purchased an apartment for me; he was my personal chauffeur, and I controlled all his money. Finally I thought to myself, *He's a small-time fool and low class.* I wanted more. I had to take this to another level. What I admired in Mama was now a joke; my desire had greater vision, and I wanted to be known, respected, fussed over, and catered too. So I began to rethink everything I knew and I then recycled everything I learned. I added my own techniques and a lot of dare.

I refused to wear cheap clothing; I would only wear silk, satin, linen, suede, or leather. Never would I wear cotton, gabardine, poly or ester (the twins). I would only shop at the best stores for my makeup and jewelry. I wore only Italian shoes and if I wore stockings, they had to be Hanes or Burlington. The more I invested in myself the stronger my need for control got.

I later met a man who specialized in selling women, better known

*Joshua 6:22 Go into the harlot's house . . . and bring out the woman . . .*

as a pimp. He had control over all the women in his stall. The women who were with this pimp would compete in making the most money for him because it would be a privilege to lie with him at night and be seen with him in the nightlife. I even went along with him for a very short time. I couldn't for the life of me come to grips with giving my money to a pimp; besides that he had no control over me. We were so much alike that we actually thought alike and made the same decisions. I learned his game plan and stepped off. That whole atmosphere was holding me up.

Lastly, I became a teacher; I became friends with some of the young streetwalkers in the neighborhood just like myself. Girls whose mothers didn't care for them; girls who dabbled in drugs and alcohol; girls who were desperate for attention, homeless, or just giving up their bodies for free. I taught them some of what I knew and before I knew it I had my own business.

I wasn't in the business all for myself. I shared most of what I had with whoever was around me, and I would always recognize the needs of the elderly and children in the neighborhood and try with all my might to meet those needs. My mom used to say, "Girl, you hustling backwards, I'm going to stamp your head with a sign that says all-day sucker." Well the Bible says in Romans 11:29, "For the gifts and calling of God are without repentance."

The money came rolling in along with the respect, attention, and being catered too. I taught the girls that sex wasn't for their enjoyment, that to keep in mind it was just business, to feel nothing, but give a feeling. I taught them to program their minds as if they were in a show, and they were the leading ladies and if they performed well they would always get a curtain call. I believe that I learned that too from Mama subconsciously. Mama never loved any man because to her it was all business; she never spoke of love in any situation.

This was my mindset for many years. It looked sweet to many people on the surface, but inside I was emotionally and physically wrecked.

*Joshua 6:22 Go into the harlot's house . . . and bring out the woman . . .*

# The Explanation of Mama

*Mama* is a word generally used by a child to call his or her mother. *Mama* is also a ghetto slang describing a woman with an "ouch" or a woman who draws enough attention to make a man want to holler. I remember growing up listening to men on the street addressing some women by saying "OOH, MAMA" or "HEY, MAMA," or "OUCH, MAMA," mainly because she stood out in a sensuous way or she had the gift of gab and knew how to answer a man. Also because it was very possible to get her into bed. She was generally well known in the neighborhood bars, clubs, clinics, and so forth.

Mama to me was any woman that I could adapt skill from. She was usually an expert at something, be it craftiness, cunningness, sharp dresser, business minded, streetwise, or she has a knack for getting into the right places or crowds. Mama could also handle herself physically. Women knew not to get on her bad side, along with some men who dared not try her patience. That's how my mama was she'd cut you in a minute. There are two sides to most mamas—either she liked you or she didn't; there was nothing in between.

Mama didn't have to be a straight-up street girl, because most of my best-learned lessons I imitated from the good girls or church girls. Mama was any woman who could add to my game plan. I don't want you to think I learned it all from my mother. I learned things from my mom's girlfriends, aunts, cousins, neighbors, barmaids, schoolteachers, church members, crossing guards, and so on. I may have run across several of your mamas too, and they may have been participants in the spirits you may now carry, even the ones I've carried.

Also *Webster's Concise Dictionary* defines *mama* as a word in the Southern U.S.: a Negro nurse or old family servant. This definition often makes me wonder how mama came from being a nurse, or family servant, to what she is today.

The latest slang for mama is now "hoochie mama." From street knowledge it means a woman or girl who dresses sensually or loosely. A female trying to be seen or one who wants attention. An easy catch, a female ready to give a play. A gold digger. A female with attitude, outspoken, usually conceited. A female on a hunt that she might feed her need, whether the need is to look good, feel good, or just be known.

Mama didn't change in her physical appearance much in recent years, but other things about mama have changed. Most mamas I knew when I was young had legitimate motives for their lifestyle; for instance they needed to pay rent or feed their abandoned children. Mamas nowadays don't need any real motives. They're just driven by rejection or something even worst. Today's mamas don't seek education; they have several children by different men. They settle for low-income jobs and housing; her aim has no real future. Mama's entire vocabulary is built around the neighborhood she lives in. Mama uses no caution with what's seen and done in front of her children. The mamas I knew had a little more privacy about what children saw unless they thought what they were doing was natural. Nowadays mamas drink, smoke blunts, play obscene movies and videos in front of their children, and even allow them to watch or sing along. Most mamas nowadays dress their children like themselves allowing no room for identity. The language of mama's children nowadays is shocking. I would have never cursed in front of an adult when I was a child or a teen, but mama's children do. Mamas nowadays let their children decide whether or not they want to go to church or school (mama, mama, mama!) and we had no choice, thank God!

I can't help but thank God for the Bible verse that says in Psalm 27:10, "When your father and mother forsake you, God will take you up."

*Joshua 6:22 Go into the harlot's house . . . and bring out the woman . . .*

# The Biblical Truth and Proof!

God gave me a biblical example of how becoming a harlot is premeditated. I also know that some prostitutes are made by force. My circumstances may be different, but my actions are the same. As you look at Tamar's situation you can see me. Let's look at Genesis 38:6–19.

Genesis 38:6, "And Judah took a wife for Er, his firstborn son, whose name was Tamar." Genesis 38:7, "And Er, Judah's firstborn was wicked in the sight of the Lord; and the Lord slew him."

In those days marriages were arranged so Tamar had no say whom she would marry.

In Genesis 38:7, the Bible says that Er was wicked in the sight of the Lord, and the Lord slew him. The Holy Spirit prompted me to look up the word *wicked*. Webster's definition of the word *wicked* is addicted to vice or sin. I believe that no addiction goes undetected by others, especially those close to the one addicted. Wickedness is considered a life-dominating sin, which affects every area of a person's life. Satan has a way of making the addict believe he/she is not being seen; however in Er's case God saw his wickedness and slew him. So I believe it's right to assume that Tamar experienced her husband's wickedness.

Genesis 38:8, "And Judah said unto Onan, go into thy brother's wife and marry her, and raise up seed to they brother." In verse 8, I was ever so curious as to why Judah had to tell Onan the same thing twice. In that time "go into," meant to marry, and "marry" meant marry. So again I was prompted by the Holy Spirit to look up the word *marry*. The *Oxford Desk Dictionary's* definition of the word *marry* is: to unite intimately, to combine to join or to give in marriage. The word *intimately* lets me know that it's more than an act of sexual intercourse. My God-given understanding of the word *marry* is to agree spiritually, becoming one in mind, body and spirit. The separation of the two instructions given by Judah—"go into" and "marry"—led me to believe Judah knew in advance his son Onan had contempt in his heart.

Genesis 38:9, "And Onan knew that the seed should not be his, and it came to pass, when he went in unto his brother's wife, that he spilled it on the ground."

Genesis 38:9 tells me a lot about Onan. First he was thoroughly clear about his duty to his brother according to their culture. Also verse 9 shows he was thinking that duty over. The Bible says that some time passed before he went in unto Tamar; he apparently needed time to plan, and when he finally went in unto Tamar he spilled his semen on the ground.

In that time it was common for parent to give meaningful names to their children, or names that described them. *Tamar* means palm tree, which is "slender" and "beautiful" in the Hebrew language. Onan could have possibly wanted Tamar in a sensuous self-centered way, because she may have been attractive. As we look further into the Scriptures this may be more relevant. One thing for sure is that he never intended to obey his father's instructions or honor his dead brother by raising up seed to him. In verse 10 God slew Onan because he did evil in the sight of God.

Again wickedness is a life-dominating sin that affects every area of life, so I can say that Tamar was affected by the evil of Onan.

Genesis 38:11, "Then Judah said to Tamar his daughter in-law, Remain a widow at thy father's house, till Shelah my son be grown for he said, lest peradventure he die also, as his brethren did. And Tamar went and dwelt in her father's house." I get the impression Tamar's presence was no longer welcomed; she could have remained a widow where she was. Judah, as the Scripture indicated, never intended on giving his youngest son Shelah to Tamar for fear he would die. I wonder if Judah knew that his sons didn't just die, but that God slew them. It also seems like disobeying God runs in Judah's family, because he

*Joshua 6:22 Go into the harlot's house . . . and bring out the woman . . .*

too thought up a plan not to honor the culture or his dead son. Again Tamar was mistreated and now abandoned.

Genesis 38:12, "In the process of time the daughter of Shuah Judah's wife died, and Judah was comforted, and went up unto his sheepshearers to Timnath, he and his friend Hirah the Adullamite." Judah having finished grieving the loss of his wife acted much like his son Onan. He no longer gave thought to their culture, but went about his business with no regard for Tamar.

Genesis 38:13, "And it was told to Tamar saying, Behold thy father-in-law goeth up to Timnath to shear his sheep." Sounds like gossip to me, although it was the truth. It also could have been the adversary pouring alcohol on open wounds.

Like many of the mamas I knew, and of course myself, Tamar had issues. Neither of us had any relationship with God, nor any role models present to exhibit God.

Here are some of the issues Tamar had. She lost two husbands, a mother-in-law, and a home. Tamar was abandoned, mentally and sexually abused; she was rejected and denied the fulfillment of her husbands' customs. She was full of grief and her self-esteem was at an all-time low.

Again the Bible says nothing about Tamar having a relationship with God; neither does it talk about Judah and his sons having a relationship with God. There were no spiritual role models for Tamar as we can see in the character of Judah and his sons. So Tamar had no real reason to turn to their God.

My personal belief is that people are a product of their environment. I get that same impression from the Bible. The Scripture says, "Come from amongst them and be ye separate." Why separate? Because the Bible also says, "Bad company corrupts good morals." I wonder if Tamar followed the suit of her company.

What has happened in my life and the lives of the people I know is that God changes the atmosphere of the mind and then changes the person. In some cases a physical change of venue is necessary, but in all cases there's a mental change. He calls us out of the world and into the church, in an atmosphere of holiness, where the character of God is displayed. As a result of this change the mind and the condition of the heart is changed and we become new creatures.

Tamar was taken out of her culture concerning marriage, but not mentally—her mind or her heart was not changed as a result of being exposed to Judah and sons. What she learned from Judah and his sons was how to go against culture, wait, think, plan, and carry out her plan.

Her background was one whose culture served war and sex goddesses, Anath, Astarte and Asherah. These goddesses were directly related to every gross sexual act ever performed, including whoredom, which brings me to the point. The environmental seeds from her culture began to grow and the spirit of her atmosphere began to dictate to her. Let's see how.

Genesis 38:14, "And she put off her widow's garments from her, and covered her with a veil, and wrapped herself and sat in an open place, which is by the way to Timnath: for she saw that Shelah was grown, and she was not given unto him to wife."

At the beginning of verse 14 the word *and* stands out. *And* has always been a word put in place as a result of something happening before it. Seems like Tamar put on some thought before she put off her widow's clothes.

Tamar covered her with a veil and wrapped herself. Putting on the clothes and the attitude of a harlot is learned. Tamar did here just what a modern-day harlot would do: She disguised herself. Tamar put on a veil; women today put on makeup, wigs, and false eyelashes, colorful contacts, and all sorts of implants. I have nothing against wearing these items as long as I know why I wear them. My sisters in the church may not go that far for fear of being discovered. Their veil or disguises are the titles they've earned, eloquent prayers, holy performances or some even hide behind husbands. No matter what the disguises are, sisters, you're still sitting in an open place by the way of being a snare to a brother.

Moving right along, Tamar wrapped herself, the Bible says. I've never seen anything wrapped that didn't bring out the true form of itself. You can wrap a mummy with cloth bands and still see the shape of the body. You can put a gift in a box and wrap it, and its form would let you know it's a box. Modern-day harlots wore wrappings just as I did. Anything that you wear that clings to your body and shows the true form of itself can be considered a wrap. So Tamar carefully planned to be seen wrapped. To make sure she was seen she sat in an open place.

*Joshua 6:22  Go into the harlot's house . . . and bring out the woman . . .*

Again maybe my sisters in the church don't take those kinds of measures but you're still in an open place; God can see you and your kind.

The Bible is clear about Tamar's motive when she sat in an open place, which is, by the way, to Timnath: "For she saw that Shelah was grown, and she was not given unto him to be a wife."

Harlots have different motives. I've shared mine, here are some to consider. Some want the world, some want money, some want attention or control, and others want to destroy what God has given them. No matter what the motive, their pimp the devil wants to steal, kill, and destroy.

Tamar also studied Judah pretty well. She knew where he was going because she was told, but she was never told what road he would take or when he would take it. The Bible says Judah went to shear HIS sheep. Judah apparently had his own business, and Tamar studied him and you can believe she knew which road he would take and how he handled his business. Believe me, this was premeditated. Tamar also had an eye for what Judah would like; he and his sons were into Canaanite women, you know.

Genesis 38:15, "When Judah saw her, he thought her to be a harlot; because she had covered her face." The plan was in motion, she got him thinking.

Genesis 38:16, "And he turned unto her by the way, and said, Go to, I pray thee, let me come in unto thee, for he knew not that she was his daughter-in-law."

Judah shows his weakness here by not talking in a complete sentences. He says, "Go to." Go to where? And what does praying have to do with it? The only clear statement he makes is "Let me come in unto thee." Believe me, sister, the girl's antennas went up; she only responded to the statement "Let me come in unto thee."

"And she said, what wilt thou give me that thou mayest come in unto me?" Here's where the cost comes in for both Judah and Tamar. Judah is asking for sex from a woman who is in disguise, not knowing or caring whom or what he is attaching himself to. Believe me, there's a price to pay for being so foolish. You give up all your rights and leave yourself vulnerable in the hands of a prostitute, as you will see in Judah's case.

Prostitution calls for more than selling your body depending on

*Joshua 6:22  Go into the harlot's house . . . and bring out the woman . . .*

what the prostitute's needs are; in other words there's a motive inside a motive. If she's a junkie she may need more than one fix. She has to fix her pimp somehow—there's always a man involved. She has to fix her drug bill—the need for drugs always calls for credit. If she has kids, she has to fix them too—children of addicts always go lacking something. Drug addicts usually live from place to place so she has to fix her living arrangements. So according to his or her need, you, the trick, may be in for more than a treat. You may get laid, robbed, beaten, hepatitis, or set up for something worse.

If she's a sadist—and these types usually specialize in violence— and if you don't know her reputation, Lord help you. Some harlots are just plain crazies; they're not out to give you a thrill but to get their own.

Her motive may be that she could be looking for you to give her a long-term payment by getting into your wallet, and this could bring on numerous problems such as ruining your credit by running up your credit card. Finding out your address to scope out your home to rob you. Finding out your place of employment and harass you for money. She could use those items from your wallet to blackmail you or even steal your identity.

However, Tamar's answer to Judah's question was, "How much is it worth to you to disgrace me further?" (Her cost was her self-respect.) "Just to do your business and leave me without a covering on a curb rotting day by day until the trashman comes. How much is it worth to you?" I don't know about any of the other girls but I felt like taking off my skin at times. Prostitutes don't give open-mouth kisses and require the men to use condoms; some think because they take these precautions they are not affected by their actions. But I know different; many a day I felt like millions of things were moving around in my body, like a pile of maggots. I would scratch myself until I whelped or bled. I would shower so much I gave a new meaning to dry skin. There's definitely a price to pay, and you can't compare it with a dollar's amount.

Genesis 38:17, "And he said, I will send thee a kid from the flock, and she said, wilt thou give me a pledge, till thou send it?" Tamar knew not to take Judah at his word from past experiences, and just as I said, there's a motive inside a motive. Her motive was "Just in case anything goes wrong I'll have some security." A kid is not of an impersonal item.

*Joshua 6:22 Go into the harlot's house . . . and bring out the woman . . .*

Genesis 38:18, "And he said, what shall I give thee?" The word *shall* indicates a commitment, and it also identifies the desperation in Judah, and not knowing what to give shows how weak he is. Tamar now has complete control. Continuing verse 18, "And she said, The signet, and thy bracelets and thy staff that is in thine hand." Tamar thought the whole thing over; she knew exactly what she wanted, and without hesitation she asked for things that anyone could identify him by. She knew a kid wasn't what she was after and that she had no intention of returning to the open place. Continuing verse 18, "And he gave it to her, and came in unto her, and she conceived by him." Conceiving by Judah was Tamar's ultimate goal and at any cost, even risking her life, she pursued that goal. It was the same way with me— I risked my life for what I thought was due to me.

Genesis 38:19, "And she arose, and went away and laid by her veil from her, and put on the garment of her widowhood." All I can say about the rest of the verse, they both got what they wanted; it was all planned. Who's planning your turn in the road, brother?

Finally just as Tamar's actions were premeditated to trap Judah, she had two more plans: one was to vindicate herself, and the other in verse 19 says, "And she arose, and went away, and laid by her veil from her, and put on the garments of her widowhood." Her plan was to never go that route again. I wonder how many saved sisters have put off their pimp (the devil) and put on garments of widowhood. God takes care of widows too, you know.

There, you have it, real proof that being a harlot is premeditated, from the Word and by my testimony.

*Joshua 6:22 Go into the harlot's house . . . and bring out the woman . . .*

# A Change Gonna Come

The outcome of all my actions led to drug addiction and depression. After a short period of time in the nightlife, my spirit began to sag. I needed something to pick me up (cocaine) and something to put me down (heroin). I also began to get very emotional because of the drugs and could no longer feel numbness about certain situations. So I began to drown my pain with alcohol. After years of drinking and drugging, I forgot about money, control, or being catered too. All I wanted was to be loved, so I thought. There was no longer a cost involved, at least not for sex. I began to sleep around, and a very heavy depression set in. I was now at the point of sink or swim.

One day I remembered a song my mom used to make me and my sisters sing outside our front door before we would eat dinner every day. It just kept playing in my head, over and over and over again. It was Sam Cooke's "Song a Change Gonna Come." Here's the part I had to sing. "Ooh there's been times when I thought I wouldn't last for long, now I think I'm able to carry on, it's been a long, a long time comin' but I know a change gon' come, oh yes it will." As this song continuously played in my spirit, I began to cry. The song played in my mind for about two weeks, and everyone who would listen to me. I would say, "I don't know what's going to happen, but I know a change gonna come."

One day I looked in the mirror, I believe I was 30 or 31 years old then, and what I saw bothered me so much. My face was tight, dry and dull, almost lifeless; my eyes were red and had big dark circles around them; and my lips were pink with dark freckles in them from drinking. Before looking in the mirror, I tried to commit suicide, but that wasn't me. As I continued to look in the mirror, I began to talk to myself. I said, "This can't be what I was born for, my life is a mess. I look sick and I feel sick. I have nothing, I am nothing. My life is just passing me by. I believe I'm dying." I began to cry, "Lord, help me, please." When I turned away from the mirror that old song we used to sing began playing again in my heart but this time I began to sing. As I sang I began to look around and I saw all these things that were so-called accomplishments. I went through the house looking at the sacrifice I gave for all these things. I went into the kitchen and saw all the alcohol I used in my after-hour spot. In my pocketbook was an ounce of cocaine I used for myself and a lot of bags I was going to sell. But I kept on singing; tears were rolling like water. I took a look out of the window at my black Cadillac Seville, and then went into my hallway, and sat down on the floor. I grabbed the phone and called a women's shelter. The voice on the phone said, "Can I help you?" I said, "I need a place to stay." The voice then said, "What's the emergency situation?" I said, "I'm abused, and I have children." (I never told her I abused myself.) The lady then said, "I'm sorry, we have no space tonight, but if you give me your name I'll put your name on the list." She also said, "Be here tomorrow by 6 p.m." So I agreed.

I then went down the street looking for Fred, who was my bouncer at my after-hour spot. Fred and his family were from Virginia and had only lived down the street less than a year.

I had never seen Fred's mother, but I heard about how she felt about him coming over my house. She used to tell him, "Fred, you should stay out of that girl's house, nothing good is going on in there." I made a habit of asking Fred how his mother was, because I never saw her come out of the house.

Finally Fred got the word that I was looking for him and he came over. As usual I asked Fred, "How's your mother?" and he said, "She's really sick. I don't know what's wrong with her." I said, "I'll make her some of my homemade soup."

In the meantime I told Fred to tell his family members that they could have anything in my house they wanted. I called some other people I knew and invited them to take whatever they wanted. I then went into the kitchen and gave away all the alcohol but one bottle I saved for myself. I poured all the cocaine in the toilet. People were coming in and out of the house taking furniture, clothes, dishes, and so on. While my soup was simmering, I went out and sold my Cadillac. I put some of the money in the bank. I then went to find myself a hoopty (used car). I bought a bright orange Ford Pinto station wagon and came back home.

There was a war going on inside me I could feel it. One part of me was filled with excitement and the other part fear, but I knew in my heart a change had come. I was drinking only a little because I needed courage to continue what I had started and to keep the shakes off.

I sent the soup to Fred's mom. I then fed my children. I began packing only what I needed to take with me to the shelter.

All I could think about was getting away from that place. I had a hard time sleeping that night. I kept seeing a lot of black shadows moving around the room. I had seen them plenty of times before, but tonight was different, more intense. Still I was not afraid. I sat up until daybreak.

The first person I saw that morning was Fred. As usual I asked, "How's your mom?" Fred smiled and said, "My mom said whatever you put in that soup, it healed her. She wants to meet you, so get yourself together and come down the street." I got myself together and began making my way down the street. I could see her sitting on the steps. The closer I got to her my heart would skip beats. I had never ever seen a woman so beautiful. Her face was like an orange-and-brown fire, or like a reddish orange sunset. So approaching her I reached out my hand and touched her face and said, "You're so beautiful, you're all aglow." She reached out and hugged me, and said, "Sit down, Cadi," so I sat down. She then said, "Is your god working for you? Because I know mine is." She then began to tell me about the goodness of the Lord Jesus. I told her I didn't believe in Jesus as God, just as a prophet, because I was practicing another religion for 17 years and Jesus being god was not taught.

Fred's mom planted much seed that day, and we became good friends, so good that I never knew her first name, I called her Mom from the first day I met her.

I later got my children and my things and went to the shelter. I was welcomed with open arms. The shelter was nice and clean, but they

*Joshua 6:22 Go into the harlot's house . . . and bring out the woman . . .*

had rules. One of the rules was you had to leave the shelter in the daytime, go out, and look for work or go to school, but you couldn't just lie around. So I would go back to the house in the daytime. My nerves couldn't take working or schooling at that time. I hated going back to the house, but God's purpose wasn't finished yet concerning that house and me.

One day I went back to the house and found some cocaine in the couch. I put it into my pocketbook then I went to my sister's house. When I got there I went into the bathroom to take a snort. I did one line, and all of a sudden I ducked down as if someone threw something at me. I was overcome with fear. I then tried to blow the cocaine out of my nose because somehow I came to the conclusion that doing coke was wrong. I just kept blowing the coke out of my nose, and I then poured the rest of the coke into the toilet. Still in the ducking position, I eased my head up to see if I could see God because I knew God was in the bathroom with me. I could feel his presence. I said out loud, "God is in here, and He's watching me."

I could feel his eyes on me, and I was so scared. I then said I will never touch another drug in my life, and I never did. Just the presence of God brings change.

My entire stay at the shelter, or no matter where else I went, I could still hear Fred's mom saying, "Is your God working for you? I know mine is." I would always ask myself, "What in the world did she mean by that." This went on for months.

I finally moved from the shelter almost a year later, into the projects. Although housing projects are known for drugs, violence, and much more, I lived in the peaceful, quiet section. I had much to be thankful for. My place was nicely furnished, very colorful and comfortable. What made that place so special was the fact that I didn't use my body to get it or anything in it.

My mother had many good qualities; one was she had a way of making any house in any condition comfortable. Her house was always nicely decorated, clean, and filled with warmth. There was always a pot cooking on the stove.

Like my mom, I learned how to create that homelike atmosphere in my new little place. It was peaceful and comfortable. I still drank alcohol, but I changed from hard cognac to wine; it kept me with enough of a buzz to maintain my responsibilities.

Not far from my apartment was the state store, and I went there to

*Joshua 6:22  Go into the harlot's house . . . and bring out the woman . . .*

buy my wine about every other day. The funniest thing began to happen: I would get to the state store and then back to the front of my door and drop the bottle. No kidding, it would happen almost every time I'd go out to get a bottle. It happened so often that I would laugh. I decided to drink some in the car before I got home because I was afraid I wouldn't get any.

One cold winter day, I could see the sun shining through my curtain; my apartment was warm and cozy. My dinner was done. I always had the same dinner every Sunday: roast beef with carrots, peppers, and onions smothered in gravy with rice; baked macaroni and cheese; string beans; and biscuits. I would have my incense burning, my favorite jazz station playing, along with my favorite bottle of wine. I had a man then who would come over every Sunday and bring me flowers or anything he thought that would make me happy. But this Sunday was different: Nothing made me happy or content so again I got uncomfortable with my surroundings. I began to look around, and this time it was what I didn't see that bothered me. I had no idea what I was looking for. So I started to cry—my man and my children thought I was crazy. I ran upstairs to pray. I reached for a prayer rug I had been carrying around for about seventeen years, given to me on my wedding day. (That's another story.) So I placed the rug on the floor. All I could think about was Fred's mom's question, "Is your god working for you?" I then looked at the rug and kicked it into the corner; I sat on the edge of the bed and began to look at my life. As I looked I thought I had been praying to this false god all these years and not one prayer had been answered. Also ever since I entered into the relationship with this false god, my life has been a downward spiral.

I can almost pinpoint the times in my life when I have cried, and I didn't cry because crying to me was a sign of weakness or defeat. However I had cried at least three times in this one-year period. This cry was different; it was a cry of surrendering that brought me to my knees.

I crawled to the foot of my bed and said to myself out loud, "I'll pray right here like I did when I was a child." I put my hands together, bowed my head, and again I began to talk out loud to myself. I said as I looked up into the mirrored headboard of my bed, "I can't pray in here! This is where I fornicate." So I got up and began to walk away, still talking to myself. I said, "What in the world do I know about fornication?" Thanks to Bertha Burke who taught me about Jesus at a young

*Joshua 6:22 Go into the harlot's house . . . and bring out the woman . . .*

age. I proceeded into my baby's room and said out loud, "Yes, I can pray in here, it's pure in here." I began to pray. I said, "God, I'm not going to call you Jesus and I'm not going to call you the name of the false god either. I'm just going to call you God. Now, God, if you're real, you tell me what your name is." Crying, I began to knock on my daughter's closet door. I said, "Lord, you said if I knock you will answer and let me in." I believe the spirit of the Lord had brought back to my memory what little I had learned in church as a child, because I remember saying to myself, "What in the world am I saying." I kept on knocking until I was banging and crying and banging and crying over and over again. I then said, "Lord, if you tell me who you are, I'll serve you all my life." I just kept repeating myself over and over again, until I finally stopped. A few days went by and I met this lady at my daughter's day care. While I was talking to her, she invited me to church. So I agreed to come. That Sunday I went to the church. I can't remember what the sermon was about, but the church was huge. It was like an old Catholic church with the colorful stained glass windows and the real high ceilings. Also the altar was very far from the pews. The only words I remember the pastor saying was, "If you want Jesus to come into your heart, come down to the front and I'll pray with you a prayer of salvation." So I began to make my way up the aisle. It seemed to be the longest walk I've ever taken. The more I walked, it seemed the farther I got from the altar. I remember mumbling, "Good grief, when am I going to get there." I finally got to the front of the church and the preacher began to explain what salvation meant. Then he took the explanation he gave and turned it into a prayer. He then said, "If this prayer expresses the desire of your heart, repeat these words after me." He said, "Dear Lord Jesus, I know that I'm a sinner." Well, in my case I knew that was true so I repeated those words. He then said, "I believe that Jesus Christ is the son of God who died on the cross and rose from the grave for my sins." I thought to myself, *Everything I ever believed before was a lie, what do I have to lose.* So I said, "I believe that Jesus Christ is the son of God who died on the cross and rose from the grave for my sins." He than said, "You need to ask God to come into your heart and change you, make you into the kind of person he intended for you to be." I said those exact words, because that was truly the desire of my heart to know what I was intended to be. From that point on my life began to change for the glory of God.

*Joshua 6:22 Go into the harlot's house . . . and bring out the woman . . .*

# Being Transformed

I was so grateful to God for saving me that I wanted to embrace all of the saints of God at church. I was so overcome by God's display of love that I was expecting that same great outpouring of love from the saints of God. With my arms open and my head to the sky, I pursued that love; unfortunately I learned that there was a shortage of God's love in the saints. My open arms were soon dragging the floor along with my head. It seems that there was really no place for an ex-prostitute in the house of God. When I first got to church, I shared my testimony with a saint who then shared it with another saint who in turn shared it even more, until I became the whisper you heard about in the halls. People in many ways rejected me, but God was still there walking me through these difficult times. Women would make known to me who their husbands were if I was around them. When I would ask a married brother a question, the wife would want to know what I said or what I wanted.

I was hardly ever welcomed in any conversations or welcomed into any ministries. I would even see women clinch their husbands as I walked down the hall. I can't begin to name the countless attacks and accusations made against me concerning single and married men in the church. For me it was one big horrible experience.

I once called a ministry leader at home about my ministry duty and his wife answered the phone. She graciously allowed me to speak with him. The next morning while I was at work I got a call from this particular woman who wanted to know how I knew her husband would be home at the hour when I called. She then went on to tell me she knew that I had a lust problem and people with these sorts of problem are capable of having sex with animals if they don't get the help they need. Well, I guess you know she ruined my day.

Another situation hurt me really deeply. I was walking into the church one Wednesday night for Bible study, and as you walk in the building you walk into the foyer. If you walk a little further you walk into the church's hallway where there's a phone on the wall. Apparently someone saw me walk in. Suddenly the phone rang; the doorkeeper rushed over to the phone and answered it. He then turned to me saying, "Saundra Robinson, the phone is for you." I said, "Me? No one calls me here, I have no family." So I took the phone and said "Hello." The person on the other end said, "You dirty bum, stinking whore, you better leave my man alone, you stinking, dirty bum," and then hung up the phone.

I can't describe what I went through at that very moment; I guess the right word would be that I was devastated. I looked around to see who was watching, but I saw no one. My heart sank, my eyes were full of tears; I couldn't stop shaking. The doorkeeper asked me what was wrong; all I could do was cry and walk away.

No matter how many classes I took or how many seminars I attended, I would never be considered a Proverbs 31 woman or qualified to teach other women anything concerning the things of God. I was a fairly new convert, only saved eight years at the time and I had a heck of a rejection issue. God's love had little meaning to me after those experiences. God's love was never enough nor did I understand it especially if it had to come through people.

The Lord took that opportunity to show me my many sins and to have me grow into maturity. The Lord showed me how I grew more in self-centeredness and took a daily swim in self-pity along with people pleasing, low self-esteem, stinking thinking, anger, bitterness, vengefulness, and wrong focus. Finally after many long seasons of tears, hair loss, weight gain, ulcers, headaches, sleepless nights, unforgiveness, wrathfulness, and so on, I then took my eyes off people and began to accept what God's word had to say about me, and his intimate love towards me.

*Joshua 6:22 Go into the harlot's house . . . and bring out the woman . . .*

I don't want to leave you with the impression that everyone in the church was against me, because that wouldn't be true. God used key people to help mold me, hold me, encourage me, teach, and direct me to him.

I remember a teacher of mine asking me, Did I know how much she loved me? Crazy as it may sound, I got physically sick because she said she loved me. For about two weeks after that I kept asking God and myself, *Why did she say that? Was she trying to be smart or something?* I can remember putting my hands over my ears because I could still hear her say she loved me. That made me so uncomfortable. Until one day I was passing by my bedroom mirror, I saw myself, and said crying, "God, why did she say that she loved me?" God said, "It was me who said it through her." Well, let the healing begin. I don't remember anyone telling me that I was loved at any time in my life before she did, and I most certainly didn't think I deserved it.

My suggestion to anyone who has a background such as mine and wants to share it with someone for whatever purpose: I suggest that you pray first and be led by the spirit of the Lord.

*Joshua 6:22 Go into the harlot's house . . . and bring out the woman . . .*

# Shall We Remain in Sin?
## God Forbid

Most of the girls I grew up with had the same mindset, which was, you gotta use what you got to get what you want. Also nothing from nothing leaves nothing; you gotta have something if you want to be with me. Their daughters grew up with the same mindset. Most young women I know believe that men owe them something because they're young, shapely, and beautiful. It's hard to believe anything else when the media is dictating to you what your lifestyle should be like along with your peers and so forth. Have you even considered what God who created you has to say?

God who created woman (Genesis 2:22–23) has much to say about his creation.

First, God knows you. In Psalm 139:13 the word of God says, "For you created my inmost being; you knit me together in my mother's womb." Psalm 139:15 the word of God says, "My frame was not hidden from you when I was made in the secret place" (NIV).

Not only does God know you, he is familiar with your comings and goings. Psalm 139:7–8 the word of God says, "Where can I go from your Spirit? Where can I flee from your presence? If I go up to the heavens, you are there, If I make my bed in hell you are there."

God cares for you also. Hebrews 2:6 says, "What are human beings that you are mindful of them, or mortals that you care for them?"

God says you're royalty. Hebrews 2:7 says, "You have made them for a little while lower than the angels; you have crowned them with glory and honor, subjecting all things under their feet."

God says that you're gifted. His gifts are without repentance.

God loves you and he wants to show you how much; take a look at his plans in expressing that love.

God in his creating of you also had a plan for your life. His plan is that you have life, and have it more abundantly.

You can experience abundant life through Christ Jesus. The Bible says we are separated from God because of sin in our lives. Sin came into the world through man's rebellion against God.

Since one man sinned then we were all born into sin. For the Bible says, "All have sinned and come short of the glory of God" (Romans 3:23).

In Romans 6:23 the Bible says, "For the wages of sin is death (separation from God): but the gift of God is eternal life through Jesus Christ our Lord."

Sinful mankind has tried to unite with God through good deed, religion, philosophy, and morality, but man can't bargain with God. It is through repentance (turning away from sin), and faith (believing), which is God's holy way.

There's only one solution to this separation problem, and that is our Lord Jesus Christ. When Jesus died on the cross he paid the penalty for all our sins and enabled mankind to again be united with God through him.

The Bible says in Romans 5:8, "But God showed His love towards us, in that, while we were yet sinners Christ died for us."

John 14:6 says, "Jesus saith unto him, I am the way, the truth, and the life no man cometh unto the Father, but by me." Ephesians 2:8–9 says, "For by grace we are saved through faith; and not of yourselves: it is the gift of God; not of works that no man should boast."

You must make a choice: either stay separated or be united with God through Christ.

You can receive Christ into your heart now by personal invitation.

The Bible says, "Behold I stand at the door and knock (Christ speaking): If any man hear my voice and open the door, I will come into him."

*Joshua 6:22 Go into the harlot's house . . . and bring out the woman . . .*

John 1:12 says, "But as many as received Him, to them gave He the power to become the sons of God even to them that believe in His Name."

Romans 10:13 says, "For whoever shall call upon the name of the Lord shall be saved."

## SUGGESTED PRAYER

Dear Lord Jesus, I admit that I'm a sinner, and I believe that Jesus Christ is the son of God who died and rose again for my sins. Lord, come into my heart and save me, make me the kind of person you intended for me to be. Lord, lead me to a church where I can grow in the grace and knowledge of God, and there I'll be faithful and submit my will in all your doings through me. In the name of Jesus, I thank you. Amen.

*Joshua 6:22  Go into the harlot's house . . . and bring out the woman . . .*

# Choose You This Day Whom You Will Serve

(JOSHUA 24:15)

For those who choose not to accept Jesus Christ as your personal savior, I have this one last set of testimonies.

I know of many women who have been killed or beaten at truck stops, in alleys, and so on. And you may say to yourself, "I ain't livin' like that," and you may not praise God. To God, however, sin is sin no matter where or how you commit it; the wages of sin is death. The Bible says in Galatians 6:8, "For he that soweth to his flesh shall of the flesh reap corruption; but he that soweth to the Spirit shall of the Spirit reap life everlasting."

The devil is the author of that death. He will kill your self-esteem, your time, your dreams, your youthful looks, your hope, and even your physical body with diseases. It only takes one sexual encounter to get HIV/AIDS.

I once knew a girl who I really got close with while on the stroll. She would teach me different things so that I would not get hurt. We once had a date together and the men wanted to just slap us around

*Joshua 6:22 Go into the harlot's house . . . and bring out the woman . . .*

a little so we agreed. That's sounds really crazy, right. Well, what can I say. My friend went first, and before I could take off my clothes the man pulled out a horsewhip and beat her so bad he cut through her shirt, all I saw was blood. It reminded me of the *Roots* movie. I can't remember if I was beaten; I have blocked so much stuff out of my mind, but I do believe I was hit, but I got away and ran for help.

This same friend of mine went one night to a truck stop; I remember her telling me, "I'll see you later," and later never came. She was found dead several days later with her throat cut. You may still say, "I don't go to those kinds of places or walk the streets at night" and that may be true also, but these things can happen anywhere, with people you believe you're familiar with. People who are driven by lust are dangerous; just ask yourself—what's driving the lust? Just think about the man with the whip—what in the world was driving him? What had he experienced to bring him to that level, and what in the world was driving us to take that kind of abuse? For me at that time it was money, but it started out as a rejection/control issue; as you can see the devil can bring you to level where you don't mind being beaten with a horsewhip. The Bible says in Jeremiah 17: 9, "The heart is deceitfully and desperately wicked, who can know it?"

I had another friend who I traveled with and the circumstances were different. We were now professional call girls and would be called for celebrities, government officials, and so on. Well, she got herself getting emotionally involved with one of the clients; she believed he would set her up for life because he would give her money anytime she asked. He called for her one weekend. I told her not to go, because for some reason I didn't trust him. She went anyway. I didn't see her for three days, and when I did her face was twice its original size. I cried so hard when I saw her face. She told me what he did to her; I could barely stand to hear it without crying. I guess trying to humor herself and me, she said, "But girl, I got paid!" She had a lot of money, but no amount of money could repair the damage done to her mentally.

You still may say, "That will never happen to me, I don't even go there," and that also maybe true. You may never have to go there, but let me take you here. Meet shame. Shame will take you places where you never thought you'd go. Shame is one of the devil's tactics. He gets you in a state of mind that gets you in a sinful action that causes

*Joshua 6:22 Go into the harlot's house . . . and bring out the woman . . .*

shame in your life. Shame then puts on wheels and takes off. First it wants to hide; after hiding it wants to come out of one hiding place and go to another, but it can't because of itself so it settles in and gets deeper into itself and when you look up you're in a place you don't want to be, and for some that's a good place to be because then you can look up and call out to Jesus.

But watch it now because shame has a twin named pride. Shame takes you to a place you never wanted to go and pride keeps you there, and there you have it—you live in a house of shame and walk daily down Pride Lane and when you get there anything goes.

So all I can say now is if you've had any situation similar to these, it's a close call, and so is Jesus!

*Joshua 6:22  Go into the harlot's house . . . and bring out the woman . . .*

# Sister Saint, God is Not Mocked

(GALATIANS 6:7)

God is a loving, kind, forgiving, and gracious and most definitely a longsuffering god. I believe the best way to describe God the way I've experienced him is compassionate. God has loved me through some really ugly times. Times when I was the woman at the well, I'd one moment be drinking the word of God at church and the next minute at home living with a man who was not my husband. God was there confronting and restoring me gently, by simply saying, "You've had two husbands and the one you're living with now is not yours."

There was also a time when I was caught in adultery; I didn't know what to do with all the loneliness I was experiencing, hormonal changes in my body, and rejections from my past and the singleness in having been through a divorce along with beginning my single life in Christ. I left the church and came back pregnant. While many stared, whispered, and pointed fingers, God was saying, "Many can point fingers, Saundra, but not one can cast a stone, go and sin no more" (John 8:11).

There was even a time when I should have been called Delilah, when I stole the heart and the strength of a new convert and left him for dead. God was full of compassion; he took me back and called me his bride. When all was said and done by man and myself, God still deemed me worthy of crying at his feet when it was clear to me that I was forgiven much.

God has loved many women like me before me. He still continues to love women the same way with much compassion and patience.

The compassion of God is not to be taken for granted. The Bible says in Galatians 6:7, "Be not deceived; God is not mocked: For whatsoever a man soweth, that shall he also reap." The New Living Translation says, "Don't be misled. Remember that you can't ignore God and get away with it. You will always reap what you sow" (Galatians 6:7).

In all of God's goodness he has another side especially for the saints of God who purposely sin against him after they have been taught his will.

"You therefore, who teach another do you not teach yourself?" (Romans 2:21) I believe all Christians are teachers whether in Sunday school or just on the streets. Wherever you go, and whatever you do, you take the light of Christ with you, and someone is always watching, imitating, or wanting what they see in you because of Christ. "Let not many of you become teachers, my brethren, knowing that such we shall incur a stricter judgment" (James 3:1).

"For though by this time we ought to be teachers, we have need again for someone to teach us the elementary principles of the oracles of God" (Hebrews 5:12).

"Therefore bring forth fruit in keeping with your repentance" (Matthew 3:8).

"Therefore let him who thinks he stands take heed lest he fall" (1 Corinthians 10:12).

I mentioned briefly how some harlots in the church disguise themselves as sisters in the Lord in chapter 3. I now want to talk more on that subject. Because I have experienced this type of lifestyle, I can still detect that harlot spirit. I don't go around looking for those ways in women, but if you've played basketball for many years you know a foul when you see one.

My sisters in the church play games with the brothers the same way I did in the streets. I see it so clearly, and I stand praying, "Lord, don't let the brother fall for that." The body language used by some women in the church when expressing themselves about the things of the Lord is mockery. I've seen women kiss brothers on their cheeks

*Joshua 6:22 Go into the harlot's house . . . and bring out the woman . . .*

and necks so sensually it would leave a wet spot on him and call it the holy kiss. I've also seen women hug brothers with their breasts lying all over the brother's chest, and I've seen sisters rubbing on brothers when talking to them. That kind of body language gives away the intent of the heart. The dress is downright sleazy and the lust in the hearts of some of the women reeks of cheap perfume on a dirty body. Let me tell you, God is not mocked. Oh yeah, I played that game too. The spanking I took was out of this world. I'm still trying to receive in my spirit the scripture that talks about God chastening the ones he loves.

Sisters, I know many women who left the church because they had been found out. How long will you live with your secret before you get help? Or is it a secret? If you don't seek help the devil will help you get found out. There's still no end to his tactics. Maybe God himself will expose you. To God sin is sin and although you may have a title or a husband or a relative who has a great reputation in the church, it doesn't matter, God still will expose you. He is no respecter of persons, and the Bible says your sins will find you out. So it doesn't matter if you sinned in the royal palace, within the royal suite on royal sheets with King David; the consequences are still the same: God will expose your royal behind.

*Joshua 6:22  Go into the harlot's house . . . and bring out the woman . . .*

# The Bride of God

God is good in all his dealings with his women. He calls us his brides. He presents himself in several scriptures as our husband (Jeremiah 3:14, 31:22; Isaiah 54:5). He's also our redeemer.

Let's look at the book of Ezekiel 16:4–15, "On the day you were born your cord was not cut, nor were you washed with water to make you clean, nor were you rubbed with salt or wrapped in cloths." Verse 5: "No one looked on you with pity or had compassion enough to do any of these things for you. Rather, you were thrown out into the open field, for on the day you were born you were despised."

I can't speak for other women but this scripture resembles much of my young life. Despised and thrown into an open field. Physically you may not have experienced anything like this but what about mentally or emotionally.

Verse 6: "Then I passed by and saw you kicking about in your blood, and as you lay there in your blood I said to you, Live!" Verse 7: "I made you grow like a plant of the field. You grew up and developed and became the most beautiful of jewels. Your breasts were formed and your hair grew, you who were naked and bare."

I believe the Lord was making sure many of us survived and grew as he looked on in our circumstances.

Verse 8: "Later I passed by, and when I looked at you and saw that you were old enough for love, I spread the corner of my garment over you and covered your nakedness. I gave you my solemn oath and entered into a covenant with you, declares the Sovereign Lord, and you became mine."

I know some of you may have asked, "God, where you were when I was going through? . . ." In this scripture God had a direct answer for me when I asked that question. He said, "When I looked at you and saw that you had enough of the lifestyle you were living and wanted to experience my love, I then spread the corner of my garment over you and covered your shame. I saved you."

Verse 9: "I bathed you with water and washed the blood from you and put ointments on you. I clothed you with an embroidered dress and put leather sandals on you. I dressed you in fine linen and covered you with costly garments."

I believe God has done something similar for all of us. This scripture to me says: "I washed you with my word, anointed you with the oil of my Spirit, taught you about my armor and then showed you how to put it on."

Verse 11: "I adorned you with jewelry: I put bracelets on your arms and a necklace around your neck." Verse 12: "And I put a ring on your nose, earrings on your ears and a beautiful crown on your head."

Verse 13: "So you were adorned with gold and silver; your clothes were of fine linen and costly fabric and embroidered cloth. Your food was fine flour, honey and olive oil. You became very beautiful and rose to be a queen."

Verse 14: "And your fame spread among the nations on account of your beauty, because the splendor I had given you made your beauty perfect, declares the Sovereign Lord."

Verse 15: "But you trusted in your beauty and used your fame to become a prostitute." Prostitution to God covers a variety of things other than the body.

Again God is good to his women and he has given us all we need to live the Christian life, spiritually and materialistically, and on some of us he's lavished with wealth and riches. Some of us have abundance of money, beauty, gifts, and talents. God is extravagant in the things he gives. A lot of women take God for granted and misuse the things he gives them. Some of us take our talents and use them for selfish gain, or take our gifts and use them against the saints of God, or use them to get favors or to give them. Many of us use our gifts and talents to draw attention to ourselves or get sexual favors. I know a Christian man who once gave me some money in a time of need and said he was

*Joshua 6:22 Go into the harlot's house . . . and bring out the woman . . .*

lending to the Lord, but he was trying to get his return from me, and it was probably because my gift of influence was being used as a seducing and manipulative spirit.

Our God is a jealous god and he won't stand for his women or his wives conducting themselves in that manner. He will identify it and deal with it. Let's look at how in Hosea chapters 2 and 3.

Hosea 2: 2, "Rebuke your mother, rebuke her, for she is not my wife, and I am not her husband. Let her remove the adulterous look from her face and the unfaithfulness from between her breasts."

Verse 3: "Otherwise I will strip her naked and make her as bare as on the day she was born; I will make her like a desert, turn her into a parched land, and slay her with thirst."

Verse 4: "I will not show my love to her children, because they are the children of adultery."

Verse 5: "Their mother has been unfaithful and has conceived them in disgrace. She said, I will go after my lovers, who give me my food and my water, my wool and my linen, my oil and my drink."

Verse 6: "Therefore I will block her path with thorn bushes; I will wall her in so that she cannot find her way."

Verse 7: "She will chase after her lovers but not catch; she will look for them but not find them. Then she will say, I will go back to my husband at first, for then I was better off than now."

Verse 8: "She has not acknowledged that I was the one who gave her the grain, the new wine and oil, who lavished on her the silver and gold which they used for Baal."

Verse 9: "Therefore I will take away my grain when it ripens, and my new wine when it is ready. I will take back my wool and my linen, intended to cover her nakedness."

Verse 10: "So now I will expose her lewdness before the eyes of her lovers; no one will take her out of my hands." Verse 11: "I will stop all her celebrations . . ."

So you see, God despises those ways in his wives and will expose you and deal with those ways. This was only a brief description of what the Lord has in store for the disobedient wife, so read for yourself Ezekiel 16, as well as Hosea 2. I have spoken on God's mercy towards his women by my personal testimony, but you can also find more of his mercy in Hosea 3 and other books in the Bible.

Sisters, God is not mocked, you reap what you sow (Galatians 6: 7).

*Joshua 6:22 Go into the harlot's house . . . and bring out the woman . . .*

# Struggles Don't Last Always

This chapter is for the struggling sister who wants wholeheartedly to please God.

"For it is God which worketh in you both to will and to do of his good pleasure" (Philippians 2:13). Don't be discouraged, sisters, your struggles will come to pass, in God's speed.

This was my struggle, and I want you to know that your trials may not be the same as mine.

While going through the transformation period, I was faced with many struggles. I had a legion of struggles, which took me in many directions.

The root of my struggles was rejection and it drove me anywhere it wanted to. Rejection would stop and hold up the traffic of prosperity; it would make constant U-turns back to old streets and park my life whenever and wherever it wanted to.

The lust that grew from rejection was my heavy weight of sin. When I got tired of being driven, or when I obtained that broken spirit and contrite heart spoken of in Psalm 51, all I wanted to do was please God. At least my spirit did. Then the battle began between my flesh and the spirit of God within me.

The first thing that happened was a spirit of desperation came upon me. I just had to have a husband. I would think that almost every man I would speak to was a potential husband. I hated being alone. I could not receive any scripture relating to God being my husband. I actually thought that God being my husband meant I would never be married. The whole concept made me sick.

I started out going to church to hear the Word, and then my focus turned to the brothers in the church. I would be disrupted during service because my eyes would roam around the sanctuary at particular brothers.

The next thing that happened was Satan began to play tapes in my head of almost every sexual experience I had and every porn tape I ever watched. It was crazy. I was completely overwhelmed. I thought I would never be holy or present myself to God as holy.

The next thing that happened was I would have sex dreams a few times weekly. They were so real I could actually feel it. I would wake up in the morning overcome by lust. I would pray but it wouldn't stop. Most of my day was a continuous battle of trying to ignore these experiences.

Then came the fantasizing—my hiding place. I would take myself to a place where everything I wanted I could make happen; what a masquerade. Then came the biggie: masturbation. I knew it was a sick self-love, but I was way out of control from all of what was going on inside me. I cried out to God to help me. Well, after all that I began to pray more intensely. I felt defeated and more unclean than I did when I wasn't saved.

The Lord then led me to identify the root of the sin, which was rejection. He led me in the identifying process by revealing some things that happened to me in my very young past. Places in my heart where deep wounds existed, places I had previously not allowed God to visit because the pain was so great.

Once God brought me through the identifying process, the Lord had my pastor do a series on generational curses, something that I had not been aware of in the Bible. The series helped me to identify what sins were passed down through the generations of my family, why I indulged in some of my practices, and whether the curse was from God or the enemy. That was only a brief description of what I learned while learning about curses.

The Holy Spirit then challenged me as to whether or not I participated in these sins because I was addicted to them, or because they were pleasurable to me.

*Joshua 6:22 Go into the harlot's house . . . and bring out the woman . . .*

I believe that the fantasizing and the lustful thoughts were an addiction as well as a curse, because I had programmed myself to imagine what men wanted sexually. The porno tapes were something that also went along with the territory. The masturbation was a pleasure to me. It was a way of relief from frustration, anger with God and others. Masturbation was also a part of what came after the overwhelming sex dreams. After I came to the right conclusions, I confessed and repented.

I remember once going through the same process with smoking cigarettes. I would smoke about a pack a week for about twenty-five years. When I became saved I began to feel convicted. I tried the Great American Smokeout—that's a day when all the Americans try to quit smoking at the same time of the year, I believe the month is November, in awareness of cancer. That didn't work for me.

One New Year's Eve I remembered some words from a friend of mine. He said, "Saundra, all you need to do is throw those cigarettes in the trash in Jesus' name." He said it so much, for so many years I thought he knew something I didn't. So that New Year's Eve night I went into the bathroom and started talking to the Lord about how much I enjoyed smoking and how it was a release for me. I then lit up a cigarette and began smoking as I continued talking to God about it. I then decided to wet the pack I had. I then twisted the pack and said, "In the name of Jesus I quit." Two weeks later, a girl I know asked me for a cigarette, and I said, "Cigarette! Cigarette! I stopped smoking." I was so surprised to find that after I threw them away in Jesus' name I never thought about them again.

The point of that testimony is after being honest with God about why I indulged in smoking and my desire to quit, along with stepping out in faith by throwing them in the trash, God delivered me. My bout with masturbation was the same; when I admitted my pleasure from it and watched my feeding factors, the Lord delivered me. The Bible says in Hebrews 14:13, "Nothing in all creation can hide from him. Everything is naked and exposed before his eyes. This is the God to whom we must explain all that we have done."

In the case of the addictions, the Holy Spirit led me to a 12-Step Program for Christians. There the Lord took me deeper into my motives and driving forces. I believe that the 12-Step Program was my greatest tool for God's deliverance. In addition to the 12-Step Program, I went for personal counseling. There I learned additional methods to wage war against my flesh.

Memorizing the correct scriptures in relation to the temptation always works. For instance when a lustful thought would arise, I would replace that thought with a scripture that would help me think right. Such as 1 Peter 1:13, "Wherefore gird up the loins of your mind, be sober, and hope to the end for grace that is to be brought unto you at the revelation of Jesus Christ." I could only do this if I had previously memorized the scriptures needed for that particular temptation. The Bible says in Hebrews 4:12, "For the word of God is quick, and powerful, and sharper than any two-edged sword, piercing even to the dividing asunder of soul and spirit, and of the joints and marrow, and is a discerner of the thoughts and intents of the heart." The word of God would always cut through the lustful thoughts.

Another method was a backup plan; when I felt a strong urge to have sex I would call a prayer warrior, one I could trust with my struggles. That person would pray me through and hold me accountable; sometimes that person would actually come and take me out of my surroundings to a mall or some other busy place or just sit awhile with me, whatever was needed at the time of the crisis. I too have the power of prayer and a personal relationship with God and know how to petition God for my needs. I make that statement so that you won't become dependent on man. I also know that the Bible says, "The effectual fervent prayers of the righteous availeth much."

I would also watch my feeding factors. Things that would provoke me into a particular sin; for instance, I wouldn't dare take afternoon naps because sure as my name is Saundra I would masturbate. I also wouldn't watch television because almost every show or commercial would scream sex. Old music would bring back old memories of things I used to do that I believed was fun. The devil would actually make me think I was missing something, so I wouldn't listen to certain music.

I would watch how I dressed, because in this case I was the feeding factor. It wasn't only temptation but motive.

When I lived an unholy lifestyle, I used to go for clothing that was short, form fitting, bright in color, low cut, and see through. I also liked long nails, lots of gold, big earrings, loud hairstyles, anything that would get me noticed.

Now God has made me sensitive to the enemy's tricks. When I'm

*Joshua 6:22 Go into the harlot's house . . . and bring out the woman . . .*

dressing I check to see if what I have on stands out, or if I feel physically uncomfortable in my clothes—that's a sure sign my clothes are too tight. If I can't make a fist then my nails are too long. I watch that my shoe heels aren't too high because that would alter my walk. If I need sunglasses on to look at my makeup it's more than makeup but war paint, and that triggers warfare. I would also write down all the men I'd come in contact with in a course of a week and would be on my mind in an unholy fashion. By doing that it would sometimes reveal what I was dressing up for and whom.

Another feeding factor to me was fear. I was always afraid of what people thought about me, and that kept me worrying all the time. I would then try and prove myself one way or another.

I also would pray to find out if I'm anxious for or about something. I would monitor myself to see what week I'm in relating to my menstrual cycle—that's important in detecting my motives.

I would also watch the seasons of the year; winter in particular would depress me because it looked like the world had died; it also reminded me of the deaths that occurred in my family.

Against all these sins my most effective weapon is fasting. I can hear clearly from God when I'm fasting. God touches me in the midst of my fast; it's like he puts my flesh to rest. I'm totally refreshed when fasting. Fasting is also my hiding place; not a devil in hell can penetrate the peace I get when fasting. I do some praying for others at that time, but I mostly read the word of God and listen to what he says.

I have a 13-year-old daughter named I'ndae, who was going through some peer pressure. I called her down for supper and she said, "No thanks, Mom, I'm not eating." Well, that made my antennas go up. I said, "You're not eating, why?" She said, "Because I'm fasting." I said, "Honey, what you know about fasting?" She said, "Not much, Mom, but I do know that every time you fast you come out different." My daughter saw the power of God working through my fast and decided to activate the power of God in her own situation. I know for a fact that fasting and praying will deal with the hard issues.

I'd also like to include another powerful weapon, which is praise. I have praised my way out of the deepest depressions, agonies, irritations, and disappointments, into the most grateful dispositions.

Praising God for me has activated the most supernatural, life-changing events in my Christian walk. If I tried to tell you about some of the

*Joshua 6:22 Go into the harlot's house . . . and bring out the woman . . .*

experiences I had and am still having with God because of praise, it would take great, great faith to believe them. Praise God!

Let me offer you a review of my God-given formula for overcoming.

- Identify the root.
- Pray to see whether it is pleasure, addiction, or a generation curse.
- Confess findings; be true to yourself and God.
- Cry out to God.
- Christian 12-Step Program
- Personal counseling
- Memorizing scriptures
- Applying the Scriptures
- Backup plan
- Learn and watch feeding factors.
- Self-examinations
- Fasting and praying.
- Praise

I pray that my testimonies and trials give you hope in whatever your struggles are, and remember, struggles don't last always.

*Joshua 6:22 Go into the harlot's house . . . and bring out the woman . . .*

# A Deeper Fear, Excuse Me,
# My Self-Esteem is Showing

This chapter is to show that God's restoration is a never-ending process and the enemy's tricks are endless.

I don't mind saying that the rebuilding of my self-esteem, rather God-esteem, is still in progress. I have days when I believe I'm a woman of God and lots of days when I struggle with my self-worth.

I sometimes still get physically sick when I think about a man of God being in love with me. That's just something I can't bring myself to believe yet. I sometimes wonder what man could see me as someone to love after all I've been through and all that's been through me, but Jesus. I still can't take a compliment from God without feeling like hiding, or this overwhelming embarrassment.

God is faithful and he is the wonderful counselor. When I'm falling apart God holds me up with his righteous right arm and on those days when I feel like a widow's mite I hear him saying, "Fear not, I am with you, I've called you by name" (Isaiah 43:1–2). You have paid double for your sins and you will be comforted" (Isaiah 40:1–2). "Since thou art precious in my sight, thou hast been honorable, and I have loved thee: therefore will I give men for thee, and people for thy life" (Isaiah 43:4). Those scriptures always lift my head. I know part of that scripture has come to pass, because I often wondered why I've seen so many women I had known die and I still live.

However, I still struggle with that particular drama, but not nearly as much.

On two separate occasions I heard pastors say in their sermons that Christian men want their wives to be whores in the bedroom. I believe they had good intentions wanting the wives to know that their husbands were lacking excitement in the bedroom. But I personally don't think imitating a whore is the excitement they need. When I heard that statement I doubled over in my spirit.

I thought to myself, What in the world was my deliverance if now I have to put on that harlot spirit to please a man of God. How could this be possible when it never pleased God? I guess the whole concept makes me sick. I know that Satan created the whore. I also know that the Bible questions us about taking Christ to bed with a whore. I thought to myself, God forbid if a man tells his wife to take on the spirit of a whore and she gets turned out. Her blood would be on his hands since she's the weaker vessel and he's the priest who watches out for her soul. So I know that imitating the whore would be inviting the devil into something meant to be holy.

Since I found Jesus I also found that there's an answer for every one of life's problems in the word of God. I believe that the men of God want enthusiastic participation from their wives, something on the line of sensuous, sexy, sanctified participation. I found just that in the Songs of Solomon. It gives instruction on lovemaking, love language, and it even says to me, Take what you know and use to the glory of God in all holiness in holy matrimony.

I believe when Rabah married Salmon, a man of God, the Holy Spirit and Salmon didn't go to bed with what she used to be, a whore, but the woman of God who she had become in Christ. The Bible says in 2 Corinthians 5:17, "Old things have passed away and all things become new." She definitely had an internal makeover, just as I had. I'm glad to know that I can one day give myself to a man of God without degrading myself.

God in his infinite wisdom showed me that he has a perfect balance in his counseling. God let me know that while all of what he gave me to write in the previous paragraphs is true, he also let me know that I was wrong in assuming that the men of God spoke in an unholy

*Joshua 6:22 Go into the harlot's house . . . and bring out the woman . . .*

fashion or with an unholy intent because what was expressed by them was directly from God.

The women the statement was aimed at received it in good grace and they understood exactly what their husbands needed. The statement was also meant for me because I needed further counsel in order to experience total deliverance and be free to participate in all areas of love in the future. God also let me know that writing about this experience was necessary so no one would think its okay to indulge in any of the devil's practices pertaining to marital sex.

*Joshua 6:22 Go into the harlot's house . . . and bring out the woman . . .*

# *Love Never Fails*

I honestly believe since God had me write the last chapter about married couples and my personal struggle, he would want me to write about my love affair with him.

I want and desire to experience more love from God than I have in my present relationship with him. I believe the love I want from God is not only holy, but also apart of his perfect love for me. I feel and absolutely know God's expression of love in my prayers, devotions, worship, and praise; also as I move about during the course of the day, I consider all of that love to be a privilege. I know and see God's expressions of love for me through people. God causes people to give to me when I'm in need, to pray for me when I'm weak, to comfort me when I feel a void, to help me when my load is too heavy, to show me understanding and compassion as I grow, to be patient with me when I'm not walking in the Spirit of God. He also has me express that same love to others. There are many ways that God expresses his love for me, but when I found out how to express my love for God in spirit and truth, my need for his love took on a new level. I wanted God to touch me physically.

I know in natural relationships when you come to know a person you spend quality time with him/her, sharing with him/her in the things they like to do, and when you decide that you can tolerate their shortcomings and so on, you become physically attracted to that

*Joshua 6:22  Go into the harlot's house . . . and bring out the woman . . .*

person. I'm speaking from an outside-looking-in point of view. Although I've been married and have children, I know I've never experienced love from a man nor have I consciously given it. God actually being my first experience with love was causing an excitement in my flesh. I thought at first my hormones were raging but it wasn't so, because after a period of time that would tire. I then realized when I was in that mood I kept seeking God for his companionship and not help with crucifying my flesh. The feeling was more of a supernatural nature than a natural nature; I knew that because it wouldn't drive me to sin. I would find myself praying, "Lord, you said you could fill my deepest love needs. You do everything for my flesh, you feed it, clothe it, protect it heal it; but what about the other needs I have in the flesh. I know that you're a holy god and I don't mean any disrespect, but how can you meet that need? You did say you're my husband?" God said I was right in wanting him to touch me or show me passion, but I didn't know what I needed or how to express the need.

God showed me the relationship I had with him in spirit and truth began to drive me in the direction I was going. My place in the spirit had reached certain obedience to him in my trials, storms, temptations, relationships; my level of patience, submission and attitude, were now at a place where he is pleased.

Concerning my place in truth I reached a point where dealing with whatever happened to me in the spirit I acknowledged his truth, respected it whether it was comfortable or not, applied his truth and my response reflected his truth, not perfectly but pleasingly.

God would respond to that obedience with a heated-up love that would supernaturally run rapidly through my body like fire and arouse me. I believe God aroused me to let me know he was preparing me for something. God never tempts us with evil so this was a holy arousing; God was stirring up my love. Need proof? The Bible says in Songs of Solomon 3:5: "I adjure you, O daughters of Jerusalem, by the gazelles or the wild does: do not stir up or awaken love until it is ready!" God is always an example of this word.

God in all wisdom shared with me that just like he showed his love through my relationship with him in prayer, devotions, praise, worship, people, and everyday living, he would fill the need for companionship through a spirit-filled husband and it would be there that I would feel his touch. Actually God said, "Great and faithful Man of

God." He would have to be great to even try to love my testimony. A husband that would live with me according to knowledge (1 Peter 3: 7), tenderly guide me in my spiritual growth process as well as meet my physical needs. He would care for my whole person. God led me through that process so that I would know his will for me as well as let me know that my manifestation of love for him through obedience had brought me to that point. God also impressed upon me that the same spirit and truth I honored him in I needed to express on a consistent basis in marriage. When I finally understood the process, all God was simply saying was, "Saundra, you're now ready to serve me in another level of love, through a husband filled with my spirit and love never fails."

*Joshua 6:22  Go into the harlot's house . . . and bring out the woman . . .*

# *Stir Up the Gifts of God*

## (1 TIMOTHY 4:14A)

### "STIR UP THE GIFT THAT IS IN YOU."

The Bible says gifts are without repentance and my mom's testimony and my own in chapter 1 have proved that. If you pick that chapter apart you'll see that I am very gifted, and that I used those gifts for evil. God has given us much, and where much is given much is required to be used. Our men suffer in the love chamber because women have lost creativity.

Use your spiritual gifts, sisters. Many women in the Bible have. Read the Book of Ruth. In Ruth 3:1–6, Naomi used the gift of wisdom to guide Ruth in winning over Boaz. Read the Book of Ester. Mordecai, Ester's nearest kinsman, used the gift of wisdom and brought Ester to a place where she could be seen and chosen, but not without first giving her instructions.

These are some practical ways to use your gifts. You may think they're crazy but you'll be surprised at what would could turn a man on.

If your gift is singing, sing in your man's ear. There's nothing like a soft sexy voice in a man's ear. Oh, by the way, sing a new song, make up words that describe only him. You're singing to God supernaturally because God is the one hopefully leading your husband in the lovemaking process. Your ultimate aim in every act of living, including the lovemaking process, is to please God.

If your man is lacking in some way or another in lovemaking and you have the gift of helps, by all means help him out. God activates gifts for the purpose of edifying another so ask God to show you how you could help. I find that people with the gift of helps are very creative and bring many ideals to the kingdom, why not to the love chamber?

You can also use the difficult situations that may occur in the marriage to enhance your romance.

If your husband disagrees with a dress you wanted to wear to church and insists that you take it off because it's too revealing or slightly tight and he doesn't want other men to lust over you, well that's an invitation to wear that dress in the bedroom to cause him to become aroused. It's the same with lipsticks; some are too glossy, they send signals and your husband may not allow you to wear them to church. Don't get offended; save it for the love chamber.

You may have the most boring husband in the world, and all he does is watch golf. Well, sister, go get some golf equipment and set up the house like a golf course. Get the golf gear, cut it up into something sexy, and invite him to teach you how to play. Also get educated with the game and just like the real game, if he makes the put give him a prize.

Your low self-esteem has no place in the bedroom, sisters. I heard many women say, "Oh, I have stretch marks and I don't want him to see them," or "My feet are ugly, I hate to show them"; "I'm overweight, I don't think I look sexy." Well, forget that, your husband isn't coming to bed for those things anyway and you will definitely act like you feel.

The Bible has the answer for that also. In Songs of Solomon 7:1, it says, "How beautiful are thy feet with shoes." If you don't have pretty feet, go and buy some pretty bedroom shoes and wear those. They probably won't fall off before the act is finished anyway.

When I read further into the verses, I couldn't for the life of me picture the beauty the author was describing in his woman.

Verse 2: "Thy navel is like a round goblet, which wanted not liquor: thy belly is a heap of wheat set about in lilies." I can't imagine what a heap of wheat looks like, but it sure sounds like plenty.

*Joshua 6:22 Go into the harlot's house . . . and bring out the woman . . .*

Verse 4: "Thy neck is as a tower of ivory." I've never seen a tower that wasn't long. Verse 4c: "Thy nose is like the tower of Lebanon, which looked towards Damascus." That too seems a little long.

Verse 5: "Thy head upon thee is like Mt. Carmel." She must have had a really big head. Verse 5 continued, "And the hair of thy head like purple: the king is held in the galleries. How fair and pleasant art thou, O love, for delights!"

I believe my sense of humor got the best of me when reading these verses. I think I laughed for about twenty minutes. However to him that description of her was beautiful and desirable, so work with what you've got. These suggestions are not meant to disregard the word of God when it says, "You are fearfully and wonderfully made." (Psalm 139:14) Nor do they excuse a husband from the practice of unconditional love.

On a more serious note, some sexual issues in marriage are complicated and need special attention. Let me offer some solutions.

- Seek Christian counseling
- Get educated: There are some excellent Christian books on pleasing your mate.
- Have "The Talk" if you haven't talked about sexual expectations in marriage. Go to a mother in your church or your own mother.
- Do a word study on all of the components of love: agape, philia, storge, and eros. The combination is needed in a marital relationship.

I recently heard an enthusiastic young preacher give his definition of love; he said, "It's an overwhelming desire to please another." Are you overwhelmed with the desire to please another? If so, stir up the gifts!

*Joshua 6:22 Go into the harlot's house . . . and bring out the woman . . .*

# The Great Commission

There's so much more to say, but I'll end with this last testimony and a challenge.

God saved my soul when I could have died with many other women I knew. I believe he saved me to show how much compassion his bleeding heart has for all women. He saved me because he knew I would, like some of the people in the Bible, go tell it from the mountaintops and in the valleys and that I could win many souls to Christ and would make disciples out of them in his power.

In 1998 my mother passed away, but not without seeing a complete seven years of my new life in Christ. My new life had a great impact on her and the rest of my now saved family. I remember her telling a man who was making a pass at me, "Leave her alone, because she has got herself together." A month before her death I asked her, if she could do it all again what would she do different. She said, "I would be a better mother." To me better had come with that confession. The Lord allowed me to share Christ with my mom and on her deathbed she accepted him. Glory to God!

I'D NOW LIKE TO LEAVE YOU WITH THIS CHALLENGE:
GO INTO THE WHOREHOUSE OF YOUR HEART AND BRING
OUT THE WOMAN OF GOD! THEN GO AND BRING OUT YOUR
MAMA, SISTER, DAUGHTER . . .

I love you, Mother, with my whole heart!

Thanks, Lord.

Saundra Robinson

*Joshua 6:22  Go into the harlot's house . . . and bring out the woman . . .*

# Questions for the Readers

- What are you teaching your children, spoken or unspoken?
- Is your lifestyle one you would like your children to imitate?
- Are you making a mockery out of the things of God?
- Have you considered your ways?
- While in the presence of men, is your mind on the things of God, and if so how do you express them?
- Is your outward appearance a stumbling block to a brother?
- Are you really abstinent or do you love yourself?
- Do you have self-esteem or God-esteem?
- Do you know any prostitutes in your church? If so have you shown them what real love looks like?
- Have you extended your spiritual gifts to the newly converted prostitute in your church?

For additional information on upcoming books, plays and poems in my series "Forty Years In The Wilderness," contact
The MightyComforter@Yahoo.com

Da' Bride of Christ Ministries
(215) 477-3467

Look for my upcoming book "Because They Knew They Could" - July 2004.

*Joshua 6:22  Go into the harlot's house . . . and bring out the woman . . .*